# Dedication

To my readers. May you always have passion in life, on and off the page.

# About The Book

***If you could be someone different for one week, who would you be?***

I'm a planner. A bookworm. A goal setter. And... still a virgin.

Growing up with a hockey-playing, womanizing, over-protective twin brother, I never had a problem with being the responsible twin.

Normally, I'm happy to stay wrapped up in my studies, with no desire for a dating life.

But this week, I have a new goal. One that will change everything.

I'm off to spring break with my three best friends, and for once, the goal for the week is all about me.

It's time to find a hot guy, spend a week under the sheets, and finally lose this v-card!

No commitment, no personal details, no strings... and no heartbreak.

I'm ready to let my hair down and be someone completely different... and when the week is over, I can leave it all behind and go back to being me.

Should be easy... right?

# Pucking Vacation

KATIE STRONG

# Chapter One

GOALS

GRACE


"Spring Break, bitches! Woohoo!" Skyler exclaims.

I flinch, quickly looking around to see if anyone stares at us as we walk into our hotel lobby. Thankfully, there appear to be enough college-age partiers making fools of themselves that we just blend into the rest of the crowd. Still, I elbow my best friend and hiss, "Would you chill? We haven't even had any drinks yet!"

Grinning, Skyler tosses her dirty-blonde ponytail over her shoulder, her brown eyes sparkling with mischief behind her glasses. "*You* haven't had anything to drink yet," she corrects. "*I* had three vodka cranberries on the plane. No... make that four. Five? No, five is too many. Rylee! How many vodka cranberries did I have on the plane?"

Rylee, my tall blonde bombshell of a friend with the most strikingly intense blue eyes, shrugs. "I don't know. I don't even remember how many rum and cokes I had."

"Me either," the fourth member of our group, Sutton, adds, her words slurring ever-so-slightly. "The flight attendant was super cute and might have overserved us just a smidge." She holds her thumb and forefinger in front of her face, the space between them minuscule. Her brown hair flops over her fore-head, the vibrant pink streaks and shaved sides giving her punk rock glamor. She is always changing her hair color and trying bold new styles, in sharp contrast to her usually shy, reserved personality.

I'd met Sutton and Rylee at the beginning of the school year at Carlisle Tech University in Northern Florida. The four of us live right next to each other in the dorms. Skyler and I grew up together and have been best friends since kindergarten, and we bonded with Sutton and Rylee pretty much right away, forming a ride-or-die friend group that I was confident would last throughout our four years of college.

My jaw drops as I look between the three of them. "Wait a minute! I didn't know you guys were drinking on the plane. What the hell?"

Skyler giggles and loops her arm around my shoulder. "Of course, you didn't notice. You had your nose buried in a book the whole flight!" She pinches my cheek and I swat her hand away.

"You guys are ridiculous," I sigh, but I can't help the grin that tugs at my lips.

"Don't worry, sweet cheeks," Skyler says. "We'll get you caught up... maybe. How many shots can you do before you start puking?"

"Okay, gross." I shrug out from under her arm and turn to face all three of them, giving them my arched brow look of disap-proval. "You three lushes stay here. I'll go get us checked in. Try not to get in any trouble until I come back, all right?"

Skyler and Rylee salute me as Sutton says, "Yes, Mom."

"Yeah, don't love that," I scold her, even though I am feeling very much like I'm in mom-mode as I gaze at their goofy expres-sions. "Just stay put. Good girls."

Skyler lets out a bark as I turn and march toward the recep-tion desk. As I draw near, one of the receptionists looks up and gives me a bright smile. I'm impressed that she looks so put together and unfazed by the chaos going on in the lobby around us. Her black vest and jacket are pristine, and her makeup doesn't have a single smudge. She's cool, calm, and collected. This is clearly not her first Spring Break.

"Hello," she says, right as I reach the desk. "Welcome to the Royal Miami Hotel. How can I help you?"

"Yes, uh, checking in," I tell her. "Gracelynn Monroe."

The receptionist nods and looks down at the computer screen in front of her. Her fingers fly over the keyboard for several moments before she looks back up at me.

"One room, two queens, and six nights, correct?" she asks.

"Yep," I confirm. "That's right."

"Alright, Ms. Monroe, I have you all set up in room 305. If there's anything else you need, don't hesitate to ask," the receptionist says with a polite smile.

I thank her and grab the keycards before turning back to find my friends. As I make my way through the lobby, I spot them at the bar, already with drinks in hand and deep in conversation with a group of guys who look like they walked straight out of a frat house.

"Oh no," I mutter to myself, quickening my pace. I reach them just as Sutton is about to down a shot that one of the guys is handing her. What the hell? Since when does shy little Sutton take drinks from strangers? That's much more of a Rylee move.

"Whoa, hold on there!" I exclaim, snatching the shot glass from her hand. "We just got here and you're already making poor life choices?"

Sutton pouts playfully while Skyler and Rylee burst into laughter. The guys chuckle too, looking slightly sheepish.

"Sorry about that," one of them says, running a hand through his tousled hair. "We just wanted to welcome you ladies to Miami."

I eye them warily for a moment and then sigh. I return the shot glass and raise an eyebrow at my friends.

"One drink each, then we're heading up to our room."

"Thanks, Mom!" Skyler exclaims as the guys finish passing around the shots.

I roll my eyes at Skyler's quip and take my shot. The liquid burns down my throat, but I refuse to show any weakness in front of the frat boys. With a smirk, I set the empty glass back down on the bar and shoo my friends away from the group of guys.

"We're off," I announce firmly, herding them towards the elevators. The guys call out goodbyes, but I ignore them, focusing on guiding my inebriated friends to our room.

As soon as we're inside and the door clicks shut behind us, I turn to face them with a stern expression. "Okay, ladies, time to rally. We didn't come all the way to Miami to get wasted on the first night."

Skyler lets out a groan and flops dramatically onto one of the beds. "But Gracie, it's Spring Break! We have to live a little."

I shake my head with a smile and start unpacking my suitcase. "Living a little doesn't mean blacking out every night, Sky."

Rylee collapses onto the bed next to Skyler, her words slightly slurred. "But you're always so responsible, Grace. Let loose for once!"

"Letting loose is exactly what I'm going to do!" I assure them. "I just want to actually make it to the pool before I black out."

Sutton slinks up to me and gives my shoulder a playful shake.

"Oooooh, is the bookworm going to go *Girls Gone Wild*?" she asks, her eyes sparkling. "Please, please, please say yes!"

I shrug out of her grip and shake my head. "I'm not going to flash my boobs at a crowd or anything, but... I do have a few goals for this week."

My friends all groan.

"Not goals!" Rylee exclaims, rolling off the bed. "Always the goals!"

I scowl at her. "Having goals is not a bad thing!"

Sutton moves closer to Rylee and links arms with her. "Boo, goals! Booooo!"

I scowl and wave my hands at them as if swatting a fly away.

"All right, enough out of you two," I grumble. "Go get your swimsuits on. I don't want to waste another minute of pool time locked in this room with you drunks."

Rylee and Sutton giggle as they each salute me and move to the other side of the room to dig into their suitcases. As soon as their backs are turned to us, Skyler slides along the bed until she's right next to me as I dig through my own luggage.

"So, you're going to do it?" she whispers, her eyes wide. "Really?"

I shoot her a look and nod. "Yeah, why not? I'm tired of waiting. This is the perfect opportunity to do it and get it out of my system so I can focus when we get back to school."

Skyler frowns and her brow furrows in clear concern. "But, Grace... this is your virginity we're talking about. Do you really want to give it to some random stranger? Don't you want your first time to be special?"

Releasing a long breath, I sit on the bed next to her and pat the top of her head.

"I just want to get it over with," I tell her in a soft voice. "I already feel so behind when it comes to life experiences. Growing up, my brother was always there, scaring off any potential boyfriends and overshadowing me with his popularity and charisma. Not that I really minded, but I'm finally on my own, and I just want to be a normal college girl for once. I want to party and hook up with some hot guy, then I can go to college and return to my regular life and my studies and not have to wonder what it would be like to actually be with a guy."

Skyler stares at me for several moments and then arches her brow. "So, what you're saying is that you're a horny little gremlin and you can't concentrate on being a smarty-pants because you're always on the verge of humping the tables in the library. So, you're going to get dicked down by some beef-head you meet here and then go back home to resume your Mother Theresa schtick. That about right?"

I burst out laughing, and I shove her shoulder. "I guess that's one way to sum it up."

She falls back on the bed and chuckles before she gasps, a wide smile curling her lips.

"What if you meet a hockey player?" she asks, a teasing lilt in her voice.

I tense up. "What?"

She sits back up. "Seems like you're throwing out all your other rules. What about rule number one? Thou shalt not dateth a hockey bro?"

I clench my teeth, a shiver of annoyance passing through me. I quickly shake it off, though, and reply, "I've spent all my life around players. Literally and figuratively. And while I have all these rules about refusing to be in a relationship with one, this week is not about that, because once it's over, we won't ever see each other again. So why bother even worrying? Besides, the chances of the guy I meet playing hockey are slim to none, so there's no point in even considering the possibility."

Skyler held up her hands, as if in surrender. "All right, all right...I just don't want you limiting your pool of suitors because of your weird prejudices against hockey."

"They're not weird," I grumble. "If you'd grown up with Carson as your twin brother, you'd probably hate hockey, too."

Skyler rolls her eyes playfully. "Fine, fine, I get it. I'm just saying, you're looking for a good time, so you shouldn't shoot down a hot guy who wants to bang you into next week just because he can skate and hit something with a stick."

I nod, conceding her point. "Okay, fine. I'll keep an open mind this week, but let's get one thing straight — this is just a fling. I'm not looking for anything serious or long-term."

Skyler grins devilishly. "Got it. Just a casual, fun time in Miami with a hot stranger. I can get behind that plan. I'll wingman for you!"

"Perfect," I reply, pushing back to my feet. "Now, come on. Get your swimsuit on so we can get down to the pool. I'm not going to find my hot guy fling in here."

"You got it, boss!" Skyler exclaims, standing as well. "Operation Lost V-Card is underway!"

"Grace is losing her V-card?" Rylee cries out in excitement, rushing out of the bathroom with just her bikini bottoms on.

"I want to help!" Sutton follows close behind, though she's thankfully fully dressed in her suit.

I groan and drop my head into my hand in exasperation. I need to start drinking, right the hell now.

## Chapter Two

LUST AT FIRST SIGHT

JENSEN

THE HOT FLORIDA SUN BEATS DOWN ON THE CROWDED pool area, cooking the bodies standing around or splashing in the pool without mercy. Not that anyone present is sober enough to care. I take a sip of my beer, set my bottle down, stretch my arms over my head, and relax against my lounge chair with a yawn.

"Hey, none of that," Tyler says. "We're on vacation. Be excited."

I glance over at the lounge chair next to mine, where my hulking brother is sprawled out. He's not looking at me, and for all I know, he's falling asleep behind those dark sunglasses of his.

"Vacation can mean resting," I insist. "You could actually use a nap. You've been a grumpy asshole since we got here."

Tyler turns his head and looks at me. I tilt my sunglasses down to stare back at him. My brother and I could be twins, with our dark shaggy hair and blue eyes, except he's three years older and built like a truck. I'm not little by any means, but Tyler is a behemoth, his 6'4" height overwhelming my 6 foot even. It's fine, though. I'm fine with not being quite the giant he is. I don't have to hold the defensive line for the Boulder Wildcats, after all.

With a huff, Tyler lets his head fall back onto the cushions of his chair and says, "Yeah, I know. Sorry. Just stressed. There have been rumors of trade negotiations..."

"Dude, relax," I sigh. "You had a killer first year. They're not going to trade you. It's going to be some other rookie. Now, come on. We haven't seen each other in months. We're supposed to be having fun and chilling. Okay?"

"Yeah, all right," he grumbles.

"Besides." I grin. "I thought your biggest concern was getting recognized and having the whole trip ruined. Doesn't seem like that's been a problem so far."

He scoffs. "I'm going to be recognized way more than you when you go pro. Way more football fans than hockey fans in the world."

I roll my eyes. "Right. You keep on thinking that."

At that moment, two girls in skimpy bikinis walk by and eye us up and down. One of them gives me a wink and a little finger wave. I respond with a half-smile and chin jerk, but that's it. I let her continue right on by.

"What was wrong with her?" Tyler asks, once the girls are out of earshot.

"What do you mean?"

He sits up and swings his feet around so he's facing me fully.

"That girl was clearly flirting with you," he says. "And she was hot, but you didn't even look twice at her. What's wrong with you?"

"Why are you getting on my ass about this?" I demand to know before shrugging. "Yeah, she was hot, but so what? Look around, dude. There are tons of hot girls here. What about that one girl stands out?"

Tyler rolls his eyes and shakes his head. "Are you a monk? What has college done to you? I knew you should've gone to the same school as me. Northshore Michigan is going to make you a priest at this rate."

"I'm still interested in women," I assure him. "Don't be dramatic. I'm just not going to ditch you on our vacation together for just *any* girl, all right?"

Tyler clasps his hands to his chest and speaks in a too-sweet voice. "Aw! Baby brother! I'm so touched. You'd give up sex with a hot bikini girl for me?"

"Don't let it go to your head," I warn him.

He chuckles and reaches out a hand to give my knee a firm pat.

"It is kind of cool of you to prioritize me," he says. A moment of silence falls between us and Tyler's eyes dart around for a bit before landing back on me. He suddenly looks nervous, which puts me on edge immediately.

"What?" I urge when he continues to maintain his infuriating silence.

He hesitates a moment more, before finally saying, "Have you... talked to Dad lately?"

My jaw clenches at the mere mention of our father.

"Not since our last fight," I say. "And I don't plan on talking to him anytime soon."

Tyler nods, a flash of understanding crossing his gaze.

"I know," he murmurs. "I wish he wasn't being such a dick about you playing hockey. He didn't give me nearly so much grief when I wanted to pursue football. I don't know what his deal is with you."

"If you figure it out, let me know," I growl. "Because I have no fucking idea."

Our dad, Francis Reece, is a no-nonsense real estate mogul who has always pushed us to be the very best at everything we do. Growing up, mediocrity was not tolerated in our household, and that included our chosen sports. However, he's not so keen on me pursuing hockey as an actual career, and wants me to pursue what he deems a more practical career path. He thinks I'm wasting my time and isn't afraid to tell me so, which really, really sucks.

"I don't want to talk about him," I say with a huff. "I just want to relax and enjoy myself and not think about how much of a disappointment Dad thinks I am."

"You're not a disappointment," Tyler tries to assure me, but I don't believe him. He remembers how our dad was before our mom died, and Tyler believes he's still that same man deep down: patient, fun-loving, affectionate, and understanding. I was too young to remember any of that, so I only know the cold, aloof, driven, and success-focused man he's been ever since.

"Whatever." I shrug. "I don't really care what he thinks, anyway."

A blatant lie, but I cling to it like a lifeline.

"Right," Tyler replies, clearly not buying what I'm trying to sell him. "You're right, though. We should just sit back and relax and not think about it. I'm sorry I brought it up."

"It's fine," I assure him, though now that I'm thinking about our dad and our fight, I'm not sure it'll be all that easy to relax again. I wish Tyler hadn't even mentioned the stupid fight, though I know he's worried about me. Still, now I'm worked up and annoyed. After a few moments, my irritation has only increased and I decide I don't want to be around all these drunk idiots who don't seem to have a care in the world as they laugh and party and take up space.

I move to get up off my lounge chair and Tyler asks, "Where are you going?"

"I'm going back to the room. I'm tired, and…"

My words trail off when I suddenly lock eyes with a gorgeous brunette standing on the other side of the pool. Her gaze is as blue as the ocean, and her shy, tentative smile makes my heart race. She's wearing a bikini that matches her eyes and shows off her slim figure and smooth pale skin. Her dark hair is pulled back into a ponytail, but I can still see streaks of golden high-lights when she moves her head and makes her hair sway behind her.

Suddenly, I don't care about the fight I had with my dad. My irritation drains away and is replaced by the urgent need to meet this girl. I can't say for certain what it is about her that makes her stand out among the sea of attractive and scantily clad figures around us, but I have to know who she is. I'm not the type of guy who believes in ridiculous concepts like love at first sight, but I definitely believe in lust at first sight, and I'm not one to deny myself when I see something or someone I want.

And I want this girl. I want her bad, and given the way she can't seem to take her eyes off me, I think that she wants me just as badly.

# Chapter Three

## POOLSIDE TRYST
### GRACE

I'M NOT SURE WHY I CAN'T LOOK AWAY FROM HIM. Even when he catches me staring and stares back, I can't seem to stop gawking. Arriving at the pool with my girls, I'd made a cursory glance around the area just to get a layout of the land and I'd caught sight of the most gorgeous guy I've ever seen. Relaxing on a lounge chair, his ripped, Adonis-like body on full display, he looks like he's walked right out of an ad for some fancy cologne or something. Even though he's wearing sunglasses, I can tell he's staring right back at me. Why can't I look away?

"Grace? You good?" Skyler suddenly asks, turning to look at me. I blink and finally manage to jerk my gaze away from Mr. Panty-Dropper, but it's too little, too late. While Rylee and Sutton are busy slipping through the crowd to get to the bar, Skyler's been focusing on me and caught me staring.

"Huh?" I gasp, blinking as I look at her. "What was that?"

She glances across the pool and when she spots the guy, her lips curl into a knowing smirk.

"Oh ho," she whistles. "That was fast."

"What are you talking about?" I sound breathless, which makes me wince.

She gives me a playful nudge with her elbow. "You've spotted a good one, Gracie. He's sinfully hot. You should go say hi!"

"Oh, I don't think that's a good idea..."

"Come on," she says, cutting me off with a wave of her hand. "Remember your plan? Your determination to let loose and get laid? I bet that guy knows what he's doing between the sheets. I'd shoot your shot, unless you'd rather go for the sexy giant next to him."

"No," I murmur, peeking back over at both Adonis and the Heracles next to him. There is a definite resemblance between the two, making me think they're related. Maybe cousins or even brothers. They're both ridiculously attractive, but there's something about the first guy that's practically hypnotized me. "I want the leaner one."

"Then go get him," Skyler encourages me. "Come on! What are the chances you run into another guy as stupidly hot as that one? Go over there and talk to him. You're on Spring Break, remember? One week of fun before you go back home and become a responsible bookworm again."

Biting my lip, I look between Skyler and the hottie several times before sucking in a deep breath.

"All right," I nod. "Okay, you're right. I just need to go over there and talk to him. No big deal. If he turns me down, it's not like I'll ever see the guy again, right?"

"Exactly," Skyler replies in a confident tone. "You got this. Now get your cute ass over there and charm the pants off that guy. Literally."

I release a burst of laughter. "Okay, I'm going!"

I turn to walk around the pool and as I start to leave her, Skyler smacks my butt with her hand. I glance back at her with a squeak of surprise and she winks at me. I blow her a kiss, and then I make my way around the pool, slipping through the crowd and keeping my eyes locked on my target. He continues to watch me as I draw near, a small smile peeking from the corner of his lip. My heart flutters and I feel giddy, the majority of my nervousness melting away to be replaced by excitement.

By the time I reach his chair, he's sitting up and lowering his sunglasses. I get a flash of his deep green eyes and I feel myself flush as he looks me up and down.

"Hey," I say, my voice surprisingly low and sultry. I'm careful not to look too pleased with myself for sounding so confident.

"Hey," he replies, his deep timbre making me shiver. "I'm Jensen."

"Lynn." I give him the second half of my name, Gracelynn, thinking that it'll help keep things more anonymous. It's a spur-of-the-moment decision that I hadn't planned on before, but strangely, I feel even less nervous knowing he doesn't have my real name.

The corner of his mouth crooks up into a half-grin. "Lynn. I like that. I'm glad you came over, Lynn. I was going to hunt you down if you didn't."

My smile widens. "Oh? Is that so?"

"Don't mind me," the giant next to him says with a chuckle. "Just chilling back here, being invisible."

Jensen reaches back and smacks the other guy's arm.

"This is Tyler, my brother. Ignore him," he tells me. "He's just jealous you're talking to me and not him."

"Oh, yeah?" I tease.

His brother snorts and relaxes back against his chair. Jensen stands up and I have to tilt my head back in order to meet his gaze. Damn, he's tall. I have to remind myself not to gawk. I'm supposed to be playing it cool and seductive. Charming. Grace might be awkward in social situations, but Lynn isn't. Lynn is confident, cool, and sexy.

I give him what I hope is a flirty little smile and say, "My, my, they build them big wherever you're from."

He laughs at that. "I suppose they do. I forget sometimes how big I am compared to most people. You can see what I grew up with, after all."

I glance behind him toward his brother, who's chugging a beer and pretending he can't hear us. Looking back up at Jensen, I say, "Well, I suppose it's all about perspective, isn't it?"

Jensen's eyes sparkle with amusement. "Absolutely. And right now, my perspective is looking pretty damn good." He gestures to the lounge chair next to him. "Care to join me, Lynn?"

With a playful flip of my hair, I lower myself onto the chair beside him, feeling a rush of exhilaration at being so close to this hunk of a man. The setting sun casts a warm golden glow over everything in sight, and I can't help but be grateful for the magic of this moment.

"So, Lynn," Jensen begins, his voice smooth like melted chocolate. "What brings you to this paradise?"

I tilt my head, letting my hair fall over my shoulder as I reply, "Just some much-needed relaxation and fun before heading back to reality. What about you and your... giant of a brother over there?"

Jensen's expression flickers with something unreadable as he glances at Tyler, before focusing back on me. "We're here for a little getaway too. Needed a break from the daily grind."

"Sounds like we're in the same boat then," I muse. "Maybe we can make this vacation one to remember."

A newly mischievous glint enters Jensen's eyes as he leans closer. "Oh, I plan on making it unforgettable, Lynn."

"I'm glad to hear that," I murmur, holding his gaze.

"Why don't you invite your friends over and hang out?" he suggests. "We can get a few beers and chill by the pool for a while."

"Sure!" I exclaim, pushing to my feet. "Hold on. I'll go get them."

I turn and rush back to the other side of the pool where Skyler, Rylee, and Sutton are still trying to elbow their way to the bar.

"Hey!" I grab Skyler's elbow and catch her attention. "Those guys invited us to hang out with them."

"Sweet," Skyler replies, smacking Rylee and Sutton on their arms to get their attention. "Let's go hang with the hotties, ladies."

"Oh!" I declare, after only a few steps. "Just a heads up, I told him my name was Lynn."

Skyler's brows shoot up and Rylee and Sutton both appear just as surprised.

"Really?" Skyler says, her lips curling into a delighted grin. "All right, *Lynn*. We'll play along, but that just means you've got to seal the deal with..."

"Jensen," I offer.

She nods. "Jensen. Got it. Anything else we should know? Any details of a mysterious or scandalous past we should hint at but then never actually go into depth about?"

I laugh and shake my head. "No, just my name. And don't mention where we go to school or give him any contact information for any of us. Especially me, please. Remember, this is just for the week. Nothing more. Now, play it cool, okay? Don't blow this for me."

"Don't worry, that's not the type of blowing I have in mind for today," Rylee snickers.

I gasp and playfully punch her shoulder. Skyler rolls her eyes with a smirk while Sutton snickers at Rylee's joke. They all link arms and saunter over to where Jensen and Tyler are lounging by the pool, their laughter carrying through the warm evening air.

Jensen stands as they approach, a charming smile tugging at the corners of his lips.

"Ladies," he greets them collectively, his gaze lingering on me for a beat longer than the others. "Glad you could join us. I'm Jensen."

Skyler takes the lead, introducing herself and the others with her usual confidence, putting everyone immediately at ease. Rylee winks at Tyler, who raises an eyebrow in amusement, and Sutton strikes up a casual conversation with Jensen about the beautiful view from the resort.

AS THE EVENING WEARS ON, drinks flow freely and laughter fills the air. I find myself drawn to Jensen, our conversations becoming more intimate, though I'm careful not to give away too many details about my life. There's a magnetic pull between us that I can't deny, and I feel myself falling for this stranger in a way that both thrills and terrifies me.

We all eventually make our way to the Mexican restaurant inside the resort for dinner. Jensen sits next to me, his knee pressing against mine under the table.

"So," he grins. "Are you a tequila girl?"

I chuckle and say, "Usually, yes. Tonight? I think I've had enough. I'm just going to stick to beer from this point onward. And water. Lots of water."

Laughing, Jensen glances toward my friends and his brother, who are already ordering tequila shots. "We need to make sure they drink some water too," he says.

I sigh and nod. "Don't worry. My girls might be small, but they can probably drink your giant of a brother under the table."

Jensen looks impressed. "Damn. That's saying something." His gaze turns back to me. "What about you? Not the partying type?"

I take a sip of the water that's been brought to me and shake my head. "Not really," I say. "I keep myself busy in other ways."

"Like what?"

"I like to read," I answer.

Jensen stares at me, clearly expecting more, but when I don't go into detail, he chuckles.

"All right," he replies. "Keep your secrets."

He gently shoves his shoulder against mine and the simple contact sends heat rushing through me. His leg presses more firmly against mine, and when he reaches for the chips and salsa, his arm brushes against mine. I'm pretty sure it's intentional.

By the time we're done with dinner, that same arm is around me and I'm resting my head on his shoulder. Our group moves onto the resort's bar, and Jensen keeps me pressed against his side.

Rylee, Skyler, Sutton, and Tyler disperse into the crowd. I watch as guys start to flock around my friends, and girls flock around Tyler. When I'm satisfied that my friends have found new people to party with, I focus on the man I'm with. Jensen and I stay a little separate from everyone, wrapped up in each other as we sit at the end of the bar.

"So, tell me something about yourself," Jensen says when we get our beers. "Something real. It can be something vague, if you want, but just give me some little crumb of who you really are."

I bite my bottom lip, unable to resist his request.

"All right. My favorite book is *Pride and Prejudice*, which I know is kind of cliche and basic, but I can't help myself. I'm a hopeless romantic at heart."

"I like that," he murmurs. "I don't think it's cliche or basic at all. It's a classic. Who doesn't love a good classic?"

We continue talking as everyone parties around us. Eventually, Jensen leans in closer to me.

"Lynn," he murmurs, his breath warm against my ear. "Would you like to take a walk with me along the beach?"

My heart races at the intimate suggestion, and without hesitation, I nod. Standing up, we leave the group behind and make our way down to the shore, where the gentle waves lap at the sand.

Under the moonlight, with only the sound of the ocean as our companion, Jensen takes my hand, his touch sending shivers down my spine. We walk in comfortable silence for a while until he stops and turns to face me.

"I'm glad you came over to talk to me," he says softly, his eyes searching mine. "There's something about you, Lynn."

"I'm glad I came over to talk to you too," I murmur, a hint of Grace breaking through Lynn's bravado.

We stare at each other for a long moment, and I can tell what he's thinking. It's obvious in his gaze, and I want it too, but I need to set some firm boundaries so that there's no danger of this week-long fling turning into anything more. School is my focus and relationships of any sort are simply not something I can afford to be distracted by. Better to protect my heart from the start and make my plans known.

"I know you're going to kiss me now," I say in a soft voice. "But I want more than just a kiss. I want to know if you'll give me an unforgettable week, Jensen, but that's all. Let's avoid making it personal. No talking about our lives back home. No strings. At the end of the week, we part ways with nothing but the memories we make together while we're here. What do you say?"

He tilts his head to the side, studying me for several moments. Crap, did I go too far? Was I too blunt? What if he decides I'm not worth the effort?

Before I completely spiral and freak out, though, he grins and nods. "Yeah. I'm all right with that."

A wave of relief washes over me. I smile and Jensen cups the back of my head, gently drawing me to him. When our lips first meet, I gasp, parting mine in return. He slips his tongue into my mouth and I completely melt against him. He starts slow and gentle. His first kiss is like a tasting, a sampling, before quickly growing more demanding and insistent. His control slips as his tongue tangles with mine. His moans mix with my whimpers as a fire burns within me. He moves his hands to my waist and grips me tighter as our kiss becomes more frenzied. That fire within me explodes. I feel a tingling low in my belly.

Suddenly, Jensen scoops me up into his arms. I let out a yelp of surprise and wrap my arms around his neck.

"What are you doing?" I ask in a breathless tone.

"There's a spot just up ahead," he says as he begins walking. "It's hidden behind some rocks. No one will be able to see us from the resort."

How does he know that? Wait, scratch that. I don't actually want to know how many girls he's taken to this secret spot of his. It doesn't matter. All that matters is that I'm the one he's taking there now.

We come upon this sort of rocky alcove against a tall bluff near the water. Jensen sets me down in a spot that's soft and sandy. The moment my feet touch the ground, Jensen is kissing me again, his touch rougher and more dominating than before. It's like something has snapped inside him and what control he had previously maintained is gone. My own desire burns hotter and hotter with each moment that passes, and I reach up to grip his shoulders, silently urging him to give me more.

His hands move from my waist to cup my face, deepening the kiss as his fingers tangle in my hair. The world around us fades away, leaving only the sensation of his lips on mine, and the taste of salt in the air from the nearby ocean. I press myself against him, feeling every line and curve of his body fitting perfectly against mine.

As our kiss grows more passionate, Jensen's hands begin to explore my body, touching me like he owns me. Without breaking our kiss, he pushes me up against the cool surface of the rock wall behind me.

I'm intoxicated by the heat between us, by the intensity of this moment. I want him with a hunger that surprises me, a craving that demands to be sated. His fingers run down my neck, my collarbone, leaving a trail of fire in their wake. My breath comes in short gasps as he explores every inch of me, setting my skin ablaze with desire.

When he finally pulls back slightly to look into my eyes, his gaze is filled with a raw hunger that mirrors my own. I draw him back to me, unable to resist the magnetic pull between us any longer.

He moves his hands to my breasts, pushing my flimsy bikini top aside. The next thing I know, he's sucking one of my nipples between his lips. I gasp and rest my head back against the smooth rock behind me. He moves to the other sensitive peak, and I'm stunned at how good it feels. I'd never realized I was so sensitive.

Jensen glances up at me with a grin.

"Want me to keep going?" he asks, with a teasing lilt in his voice.

I bite my bottom lip and nod. Chuckling softly, he kisses a trail down my chest and belly and drops to his knees in front of me. I stare down at him as he slides my bikini bottoms down my legs. Instinctively, I press my thighs together. I've never been in this situation with a man before, and I can't quite fight my shyness.

Jensen holds my legs, looks up at me, and growls, "Open them."

His commanding tone electrifies me and I obey him without hesitation. As I watch a sultry smirk cross his face. "Good girl."

There is something about the way he commands me that makes me want to bend to his every whim. Like a cosmic connection that has slowly awakened a deeper part of me that has longed to submit to a man. A man like him.

Lowering his head between my legs, he drags his tongue along the edges of my opening before he wraps his lips around my clit, sucking hard. The sensation is something I have never felt before and as a rush of pleasure cascades across every nerve of my body, I cry out. My fingers tear at the locks of his hair, ensuring that he can't get away.

"Oh my God!" I exclaim. "Jensen!"

He doesn't give up. He licks my pussy with wild abandon, his tongue driving me crazy. As one hand grips my hip, pinning me in place, his other moves to my opening, slowly slipping a finger inside me without warning. A shriek escapes my throat as I shove my fist into my mouth to muffle the noise. Jensen is unrelenting as he continues to pump his finger in and out of me while he ravages my clit with ravenous hunger.

"Holy shit!" I gasp. "Jensen, I'm going to cum..."

My words seem to stop him in his tracks as he lifts his head, stealing the pleasure away from me. I gasp. "Jensen, what are you...?"

"Say *please*," he says, with an infuriating grin on his gorgeous face.

"Seriously?" I moan. He winks at me and kisses just above my clit, but doesn't go lower, which makes me whimper, "Please, Jensen. Please make me cum."

With a satisfied grunt, he goes back to work on my aching core. Fingers pumping, lips sucking, tongue lapping. It's so good, and I'm so close. I just need a little bit more. Finally, I can't take it anymore and I beg again, "Jense, please...please let me cum."

He grins up at me — a look of pure masculine satisfaction — as his fingers continue to work me.

"You want to cum, baby?"

I nod and plead, "Yes, God, yes!"

"All right," he snarls. "Cum for me."

The moment I get his permission, my body explodes. My head is thrown back as a guttural scream of ecstasy escapes my lips, my mind slowly praying that the crashing waves are able to drown out the sound of my pleasure. Otherwise, God knows who would find me like this.

He draws my orgasm out until it's almost unbearable, but before I can say anything, he surges to his feet and cups my ass, lifting me up as I wrap my legs around his waist. He presses my back to the side of the rocky bluff as his fingers dig into my skin. The way in which he manhandles me as if I weigh no more than a feather causes my heart to race with anticipation.

"You ready?" he asks with a growl.

"Yes," I reply breathlessly and without hesitation—y mind a racing stream of what ifs, as I realize that in only a moment I won't be the virgin girl I once was, but a woman that has finally experienced a taste of freedom I have longed for. He pauses and pulls a condom from the pocket of his trunks. I furrow my brow.

"Have you had that the whole time?" I ask.

He grins and shrugs.

"And you thought you were getting lucky?" I tease.

He chuckles. "I wanted to be prepared for any possibility."

He maneuvers us so that he can put the condom on. Lining his cock up with my entrance, he pushes into me in one swift, hard motion. I bite back my yelp of pain as he unknowingly rips through my virginity. I don't want him to know, though. I don't want him to treat me any differently than he would any other one-night stand.

"You feel amazing," he groans, the delight in his voice making me smile. His head resting on my shoulder, his breaths coming out in heavy pants as he attempts to hold on to the last strings of control.

I cling to him, overwhelmed by the feeling of fullness and

the dull pain throbbing through me. My mind becomes a warped tunnel of acceptance as his eyes finally find my own once more just before his lips descend upon mine with another searing kiss. The kiss distracts me from the worst of the pain, and the more he pumps in and out of me, the more my body relaxes and the pleasure begins to take over my senses. Burying my face against his neck, I attempt to muffle my cries. But it isn't long- lived, as he reaches between us and begins rubbing my clit in tight, hard circles, causing me to grow wetter and wetter. The remaining twinges of pain instantly dissipate, replaced by pure pleasure.

"Jensen, don't stop," I beg. "Please, don't stop."

He holds me tighter, his hips pistoning into me with relentless pleasure as my core tightens around him causing me to explode in utter ecstasy. I cry out, unable to stop myself, and moments later, Jensen releases a muffled roar as his body jerks and trembles against mine.

It takes us both several long moments to come back down to earth. When we do, he looks down at me with a smile, gently pushing the hair off my sweaty forehead. A grin spreads on both of our lips as our breaths come out short and hollow.

Mind-blowing sex on a beach with a near-stranger. *Lynn is off to an excellent start,* I think, and I wonder what else she'll get up to as the week continues on.

"That was fucking fantastic," he says, his voice rumbling in his chest.

I nod, momentarily speechless as my body continues to hum with the aftershocks of what we just did. He slowly pulls out, removes the condom without looking, and tosses it away.

Suddenly, he gives me a mischievous grin. "We should clean up."

I furrow my brow in confusion.

"How?" I murmur. My arms and legs are still wrapped around him and I hug him tight.

Before I fully comprehend what he's doing, he turns and runs toward the ocean. I let out a yelp of surprise as we splash into the cool waters. He laughs and kisses me, holding me close and I cling to him in turn, all other thoughts vanishing from my head as I focus solely on Jensen.

As I look into his eyes and think about what we just experienced, something deep within me tells me this is only the beginning... and I can't wait for what comes next.

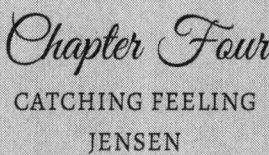

# Chapter Four

## CATCHING FEELING
### JENSEN

OVER THE NEXT FEW DAYS, I SPEND NEARLY EVERY waking moment with Lynn. I can't say for certain what it is about her that I find so irresistible compared to other girls, but when she's around, the rest of the world seems to fade away.

Tyler gives me grief on the second day of our trip when I tell him I have plans with Lynn.

"You realize we're on this vacation to spend time together, right?" he teases. "You weren't supposed to ditch me for some pretty girl you just met."

I glance over at him. He's sitting on the couch in the living room of our two-bedroom suite, one leg crossed over the other knee, flipping through his phone with a stupid grin on his face. He might be annoyed, but he's also amused. Turning from the mirror I'm inspecting my reflection in, I shoot him a grin. "Is my big brother jealous?" I tease.

He glances up from his phone. "Just pointing out a fact."

I chuckle and hold up my hands. "Okay, okay, I get it. I'm sorry. I didn't mean to ignore you or ditch you. I just... like her, you know?"

Tyler snorts. "Yeah, sure, I know, and I'm a big boy. I can entertain myself. I'm just fucking with you. It's just been a minute since we were able to hang out."

"I know," I assure him. "How about this? You and I have breakfast together every morning. That way we have definite time we're spending together. Does that sound good?"

He stares up at me for several moments before giving me a curt nod. "Yeah. That'll work. Now get out of here. You're bugging me."

Chuckling, I shake my head and hurry off to meet up with Lynn.

What stuns me about her is that I don't get bored with her. At all. Even though we're spending so much time together, I find myself wanting more. Lynn is like a breath of fresh air, bringing excitement and spontaneity into my life. As we explore Miami together, every moment with her feels like an adventure waiting to happen.

And the sex... good lord, is the sex amazing. She's made me insatiable, and I can't help but try and get her naked every chance I get.

ONE EVENING, I take her out to dinner at a seafood restaurant that's quite a bit fancier than the clubs and fast casual eats that most Spring Breakers frequent. I want this night to be a little special, though. A little bit elevated. A little bit romantic.

"Wow," she says as we are led to our table. "This is snazzy."

I chuckle. "Snazzy? Are you eighty years old?"

She flips her hair and gives me a saucy little grin. "I am, but don't I look fabulous for my age?"

"Gorgeous," I reply. "Absolutely gorgeous."

Her cheeks flush as she takes her seat and she looks down at the menu, seeming suddenly shy. I find it adorable whenever these nervous moments overtake her — most of the time, she's so self-confident. Our conversation is light as we order and then get our appetizers.

"So, why are you wining and dining me tonight?" she asks over a plate of fresh calamari.

"I wanted to show you a good time," I answer.

"You've only *been* showing me a good time," she insists. "But why so fancy?"

I shrug. "I guess I just wanted to take you out. Give you an actual date experience amidst the week of debauchery."

Her smile is bright and the urge to get to know her better bubbles up within me. I've been fighting that urge since our first night when she insisted she only wanted one week, but I can't help but want to unravel her secrets and get inside her head. If I can just get to know something, *anything* that means something to her, I think I could be satisfied.

"What are you thinking about?" she asks, breaking through my wandering thoughts.

I blink up at her. "Huh? Oh! Nothing. I was, uh, just wondering what your favorite color is."

She furrowed her brow with a confused grin. "What? My favorite color?"

I nod. "Yeah. It's nothing that will identify you after this week, will it?"

She chuckles and shakes her head. "I suppose not. All right. My favorite color is green. What's yours?"

"Blue," I say, relieved that she answered my question so willingly. What I don't tell her is that until this week, my answer used to be red, but the deep ocean blue of her eyes has made me change my mind.

"Okay, my turn." She props her elbows on the table and rests her chin in her hands. "What's your favorite movie?"

"*Dumb and Dumber*," I admit.

She looks surprised. "Really? I can't decide if I'm shocked or not."

"All right, what's yours?" I insist.

"*Pretty Woman*," she sighs. "Every time Richard Gere rolls up to Julia Roberts' apartment in the white limo, I go all gooey inside."

She probably doesn't think it's a big deal to tell me this, but every small detail about herself that she offers feels like a gift. I want more, but I know if I get greedy, she'll pull back and might decide to end things between us early. I don't want to risk that, so I don't delve any further.

As the night goes on, our dinner continues and we enjoy some more light conversation focused mostly on our time in Miami so far. It's safe territory for us and I keep myself in check. After dinner, we go strolling through the bustling streets of Wynwood, lined with twinkling lights and echoing laughter, when Lynn suddenly grabs my hand and pulls me into a hidden alleyway. Surprised but exhilarated, I follow her without question.

The alleyway is dark and narrow, the only light coming from a flickering lamppost at the entrance. Lynn pushes me against the cold brick wall, her eyes sparkling mischievously in the dim light. Without a word, she crashes her lips onto mine, her hands roaming freely over my body.

"What are you doing?" I ask with a low chuckle.

She looks up at me and puts a finger to her lips.

"You can't make too much noise," she says. "The people at the restaurant around the corner might hear you."

Before I figure out what her intentions are, she squats down in front of me and unzips my pants.

"Fuck," I gasp when she pulls out my cock and gives it a few firm strokes.

Looking up at me, she grins before wrapping her lips around the head and sucking my length into her mouth. *Shit, she's good at this*, I think, but at the same time, I can tell she's not that experienced. I cup the back of her head and guide her as she bobs up and down along my cock.

The world around us fades away as pleasure runs through me. She drags her tongue on the underside of my cock and reaches up to cup my balls. I grip her hair, unable to stop myself, and hold her still while I take over and thrust into her mouth. She gags but looks up at me with a scorching heat in her eyes. Tears slip down her cheeks. Gripping my thighs, she holds me tight as I continue to fuck her mouth.

"Relax your jaw, baby," I tell her when she starts to tense. "Breathe through your nose."

She obeys and relaxes, and before long, I'm on the edge of release. I move faster and she takes me with little difficulty. As I cum, I hold her against me and pump into her throat. She swallows everything I give her. When I finally pull my softening cock from her mouth, she grins up at me and smacks her lips, clearly proud of herself. I gently brush her tears away with my thumbs as I gaze down at her, my heart hammering in my chest.

I pull her to her feet and kiss her, tasting myself on her tongue. I'm ready to continue, but a voice suddenly booms from the end of the alleyway.

"Hey! What are you two doing back here?"

Startled, we pull apart to see a burly security guard staring at us with a mixture of shock and disapproval. Lynn giggles nervously while I clear my throat, trying to come up with an explanation.

Before I can speak, the security guard shakes his head and points back towards the street. "You can't be back here. It's not safe. Now get out of here before I have to call the cops."

Embarrassed but exhilarated, Lynn and I quickly make our exit, laughing as we stumble back onto the brightly lit street. As we walk away hand in hand, I realize that with Lynn by my side, every moment truly is an adventure waiting to happen.

How am I supposed to just walk away from her at the end of the week?

◈

Four days into the trip, Lynn's friends reclaim her, declaring they are having a girls' night and I'm not invited. As much as I want to spend more time with her, I know I've been monopolizing her so I don't complain. I decide since the girls are going out together, Tyler and I can spend the evening out together as well.

We decide to hit up a local club that Tyler heard about from some other Spring Breakers. It'll be nice to go out, have some drinks, and just hang out with my brother, even if I know I won't be able to stop myself from thinking about Lynn the majority of the time.

Freshly showered, I'm getting dressed when my phone suddenly starts to buzz. I pick it up off the dresser it's resting on, and smile when I see it's my friend and teammate, Carson Monroe. He might be a freshman, but he's already proven himself on the ice. He's one hell of a player.

Answering the call, I say, "Yo, Monroe. What's up?"

"Hey Reece," he replies. "How's Miami?"

"Great." My mind instantly flashes to Lynn, and warmth seeps through me. "Really great. Tyler and I are just getting ready to go out."

"Oh, I won't keep you," he assures me. "I was just wondering if you've heard anything about our training schedule when school starts back up? I know when we're supposed to start, but do you know if we're going right into strength training, or if Coach is going to want us to work more on endurance first? I want to get a jump on whatever we're doing."

I chuckle. This kid is impressive. Even when we're supposed

to be on break, his mind is still on the game and improving himself however he can.

"Sorry, man," I tell him. "I haven't heard yet. You've got that workout sheet Coach gave us, though, right? You can use that in the meantime."

He sighs. "Yeah, I know. I just don't think it's challenging enough."

"You're supposed to be on Spring Break," I tease him. "Relax, dude."

He laughs. "That's never been one of my strong suits, bro. My sister and I have that in common. Ironically, she's actually off enjoying herself in Miami, too. Apparently, it's where all the cool kids are."

"Yeah. It's a popular place."

"For sure," he says. "All right, sorry to bug you. Go out and get wild."

"No worries," I assure him. "If I hear anything, I'll let you know. Talk soon."

I hang up the call, tuck my phone into my pocket, check my reflection one more time, and head out of my room to spend a night on the town with my brother.

"So, you and Lynn are spending a lot of time together," Tyler says, the low thump of the club's music acting as background to our conversation. "I thought you said it was just a fling."

"It is," I tell him with a frown. "What makes you think it's not?"

We're at the club, tucked away in a rounded booth in a shadowed corner, away from the crowded dance floor, music, and bar. Thankfully, we're able to afford bottle service so we don't have to try and fight our way into getting a drink.

Tyler takes a sip of his tequila and tonic, his eyes scanning the crowded club for a moment before returning to me. "Come on, man. I know you better than anyone. I can see it written all over your face," he says, his voice serious despite the loud music surrounding us. "You've caught feelings for her, haven't you?"

I shift uncomfortably in my seat, avoiding his gaze as I swirl the glass of whiskey in my hand.

"Of course not," I insist. "That would be a stupid thing for me to do. She's made it clear what she wants, and what she doesn't. At the end of the week, we part ways, and that's it."

"Is that really what *you* want?"

I furrow my brow and shake my head. "What are you getting at? I'm having fun with her. That's all this is."

He scoffs. "Please, I've never seen you act like this with a woman before."

"Act like what?"

"Like a love-struck puppy."

I roll my eyes. "Shut up."

He shrugs. "It's true. It seems like you got it pretty bad for this girl."

"We've only known each other for a few days."

"Why does that matter? If you connect with someone, you connect with them. End of story."

I release a frustrated breath. Why is he pushing this? Why is he insisting that there's something more between me and Lynn when there isn't?

"Look, I like her," I tell him. "I like her a lot. We're having a ton of fun. She's beautiful, sexy, and sweet. Maybe if the situation was different..."

I trail off, thinking of all the ways Lynn and I just fit together. Then, with a deep breath, I admit the truth. "She gets me," I murmur. "She's easy to talk to. She's funny and laughs at my jokes. The sex is... unbelievable, and the way she fits in my arms...it's like she was made for me."

I blink, realizing too late that I was rambling. I look over at Tyler, who's watching me with an arched brow.

"Damn," he murmurs. "It sounds like you're falling in love with this girl."

I shake my head. "No...no, that's not possible..."

However, the thought of walking away from Lynn at the end of the week makes my stomach twist painfully. Maybe Tyler is right. There's a small voice in the back of my head telling me that one week with Lynn is not going to be enough.

# Chapter Five

LAST NIGHT

GRACE

"OH MY GOD, JENSEN," I MOAN, ARCHING MY BACK AS I grind my hips against him. "This feels so good."

We're in his suite, and I'm riding him as he clings to my hips. I brace my hands on his wide chest and throw my head back as my clit rubs against him, sending shockwaves of pleasure rushing through me.

"That's right, baby," he growls. "Ride that fucking cock."

He smacks my ass and pumps his hips up to meet mine. Sweat glistens along my forehead and my breathing is ragged, but I don't want this to stop. He cups one of my breasts and squeezes it, then pinches my nipple. I love how rough he is with me. How dominating. It's the sexiest thing I've ever experienced in my life.

Jensen's gaze locks onto mine, his eyes filled with hunger and desire. I can't help but return his gaze with equal fervor, my heart racing wildly as I cling to him.

"I'm going to cum!" I gasp. "Please, Jensen, can I cum?"

My body has gotten used to following his commands. It's like he's brought out this naturally submissive side of myself. A side that craves dominance and direction. That's eager to please and obey.

"Do it, gorgeous," he snarls. "Cum for me. Right now."

He reaches down and presses his thumb against my clit.

I throw my head back, biting my lip as I explode. I shake and writhe above him, tears pricking the corners of my eyes as the pleasure becomes almost unbearable.

His grip on my hips tightens as he lets out a guttural roar and cums as well. He holds me with such force that I know I'm going to have bruises from his fingertips. I love it, though. He makes me feel wild and unrestrained, and I'm on the verge of growing addicted to this feeling.

When I can't take anymore, I collapse onto his chest. For a long moment, we simply lie there, our bodies still connected, our hearts pounding in unison. A slow smile spreads across Jensen's face, and he pulls me down into a kiss, our lips meeting passionately.

As we pull apart, I can't help but feel cold without him. We slowly disentangle ourselves from each other, and after he removes his condom, I lay my head on his chest, listening to the steady thud of his heartbeat, soaking in the warmth and contentment of our afterglow.

"That was amazing," I whisper, my eyes still closed.

"Yeah, it was," he groans, reaching over and looping his arm around my waist. He pulls me against him and holds me. I love how readily he cuddles me. I didn't realize how much I'd enjoy this level of intimacy. "I can't believe this is our last night."

My heart twists and I snuggle closer to him, trying to ignore the sadness that threatens to overwhelm me. My friends and I are flying home tomorrow. My week with Jensen is coming to an end. It's been so fun and I've loved every moment of our time together. This was exactly what I wanted, but now it's almost over. The realization is a gut punch.

"I think the girls are going to have a hard time leaving," I murmur in a teasing tone, trying to deflect from my own aching heart. "They've been having the times of their lives."

They've been so understanding of my spending so much time with Jensen. Skyler, Rylee, and Sutton have been keeping themselves occupied with days on the beach and nights at the clubs. Skyler hooked up with not one, but *two* semi-professional soccer players —at the same time. Rylee won a wet t-shirt contest, which doesn't surprise me because her tits are immaculate, and Sutton got drunk on black rum and danced on a bar. I'm pretty sure they haven't missed me too much.

"Hey, I've been thinking," Jensen says, his tone casual, but that kind of forced casual that people use when they don't want something that's a big deal to seem like a big deal. "I know you said you only wanted one week, but would it be so bad if we kept in touch?"

I look up at him, blinking. "What?"

He shrugs his shoulders as he glances down at me. "I mean, really, is it that big of a deal? We can just stay in touch. Keep it casual. No stress or expectations."

His words are communicating one thing, but the tension in his shoulders and the eagerness in his gaze tells me he's not just thinking of keeping things casual between us. He wants more.

"I...I thought we agreed this was just a one-week thing," I whisper.

"I know," he assures me. "And I was totally okay with that when you laid it out for me. You have to admit, though, we're pretty good together. I, uh, I wouldn't mind keeping this going in some capacity."

I don't respond right away. Mostly because I don't know what to say. A part of me agrees with him. It does seem like a waste just to walk away from this. I remind myself, though, that this is so special *because* it has an expiration date. We aren't taking a moment with each other for granted because we both know our time is short. Still, I can't say I'm not tempted. I'm genuinely sad that I'm never going to see Jensen again, and if I just say yes to his suggestion, I won't lose this connection with him.

He drops a kiss on my forehead, pulling me from my spiraling thoughts.

"You don't need to answer now," he says, his voice gentle. "Sleep on it. Think about it. Let's just enjoy what we have left of this night together."

"Okay," I say.

Jensen trails his fingers up and down my arm. "I'm so glad I met you, Lynn."

"I'm glad I met you too, Jensen."

I am glad. Truly, and it guts me that I'm leaving tomorrow. A part of me wants to give into temptation and say that I'll stay in touch with him, but I remind myself why I set the week-long limit to begin with. This isn't really me. When I go back to college, I'm going to need to focus back on my studies. School needs to be my priority. I've worked too hard and too long and sacrificed too much to let a simple fling throw me off course now.

Jensen and I wouldn't work in the real world. We'd be long-distance because I doubt he's anywhere in Michigan, and I know the chances of a long-distance relationship working under the best of circumstances are low. Besides, he doesn't really know me. He knows Lynn, the wild and adventurous girl who spent a week throwing caution to the wind. But Grace, the girl with her nose in a book or computer, with the overprotective brother who has pretty much prevented her from ever having a relation-ship... that's a girl he doesn't know. And in the real world, one he probably would never look twice at. There are simply too many risks for me to take, and I knew this going into it. Which is why I have to follow my plans.

Within minutes, his breathing grows deep and even. He's asleep. I wait a little while longer to make sure he's in a deep sleep before I work my way out from the safety and comfort of his arms and sit up.

Gazing down at Jensen, I pause and commit his sleeping face to memory.

I need to go back to my life. I need to focus on school. I can't let myself be distracted by a gorgeous guy who even in the best-case scenario I would rarely, if ever, get to see. Any attempt at a real relationship would fail because this week hasn't been real life. It's been a vacation. A fantasy.

A dream.

Even though it breaks my heart to do so, I slip further away from him and quickly get dressed. It's better to end things cleanly and thoroughly. Shut and lock the gate between us, keep it impossible for us to reconnect, so I'm not tempted to go back through it.

I tiptoe across the bedroom and allow myself one final glance at him before shutting the door firmly behind me.

As I hurry out of the suite and walk down the hotel hallway, I feel a sense of satisfaction and pride rise up within me, and it manages to dampen the heartache I'm feeling at leaving Jensen behind. I did it. I came to Miami intent on having a memorable weekend where I let myself be wild and simply have fun. I also lost my virginity in, quite possibly, the best way imaginable, with an amazing guy. And while I'll miss him and will likely sometimes wonder where his life has taken him, I'll also be forever grateful to him. I'm returning to my regular life a little more worldly, a little more experienced, and with no regrets about anything that happened.

I couldn't have asked for a better end to my Spring Break than that.

# Chapter Six

## GONE
### JENSEN

I BLINKED OPEN MY EYES, A SMILE ALREADY ON MY face. Damn, I slept well. Truth be told, since meeting Lynn, I've been sleeping like a baby every night. That was yet one more reason I couldn't bring myself to cut things off with her completely.

Rolling over, I expect to find her nestled next to me in the bed, but I'm met with an empty pillow and a cool mattress. She's gone.

Shooting up, I scramble out of bed and look around to see if her clothes are still scattered on the floor. "Lynn?" I call out, yanking open the bedroom door and stumbling out into the suite's common areas. "Lynn? Where are you?"

Silence.

"No," I murmur, shaking my head. "No, no, no, no."

I turn and run back into my room, quickly get dressed, and reemerge with every intention of tearing through the resort to find her. As I pass by the kitchen area, though, a piece of paper sitting in the middle of the counter catches my eye. I snatch it up and see that it's a note. A note from Lynn.

. . .

*Jensen,*

*I'm sorry to do this. I wish it could be different, but I think this is the best, cleanest way to end things. I'm truly grateful to have met you and spent this week with you. You've given me an amazing experience and I'll never forget our time together, but we both know whatever is between us wouldn't survive in the real world. I hope you can understand and someday forgive me for leaving without a proper goodbye. It would be too hard and I would be too tempted to stay with you. It's better this way. Trust me. Goodbye, Jensen, and thank you again.*

*Lynn*

I STARE DOWN at the note, stunned. That was it? No number or email? Not even a last name I can use to find her?

It's just over?

No, there still had to be a chance.

Crumpling the note up, I toss it in the trash and dart toward the suite's door. Before I can open it, though, I hear heavy footsteps behind me and glance back in time to see Tyler stepping out of his room. He's showered and dressed and gives me a surprised, raised-brow look.

"Where are you going?" he asks. "Aren't we getting breakfast?"

"Sorry, I have to catch Lynn before she leaves," I tell him. "I'll explain everything later."

"She's gone, bro."

I freeze, my hand squeezing the doorknob as I grit my teeth. Turning back to my brother, I ask, "Gone? What do you mean, gone?"

"They left for the airport," he informs me. "About an hour ago, actually."

My heart is racing and I'm suddenly nauseous.

"Her plane already left?" I murmur, as I stare at my brother.

He gives me a sympathetic look and nods. "Yeah. I saw the girls leaving when I was out for my run this morning. They were loading up into a cab. I stopped to say hi...or, I guess, bye."

"What did Lynn say?" I whisper. "Anything?"

Tyler scratches the back of his neck, looking uncomfortable.

"Tyler," I snap. "Tell me. What did she say?"

Sighing, he finally says, "She said she was sorry and that she hopes you understand. She said that it was only supposed to be a week. Nothing more."

*Nothing more.* I guess I should've taken her at her word. Last night, though, I'd felt a glimmer of hope that she felt the same way I did. I guess I was wrong. Making my way back across the room, I reach the couch and drop down onto the cushions.

Tyler approaches me cautiously and asks, "You okay?"

I stare at the wall in front of me and slowly shake my head. "I'm not sure that I am. I... I really like her, Tyler, but she didn't even leave me a phone number."

Standing behind the couch, he reaches down and gives my shoulder a firm pat.

"I know it's hard," he says. "She was a cool girl and you two were good together, but she was upfront with you about what she wanted. You can't be upset with her about leaving. She always told you she would."

"I know," I whisper. "I know, you're right. Still... this really sucks."

"Yeah," Tyler sighs. "I know."

He pats my shoulder again and then walks away, leaving me alone with my disappointment and heartbreak. I wish she'd given me a chance. I could've proven just how good we could be together.

It's too late, though. She's gone, and I'm never going to see her again. Our week together was just a fling, but I know with a certainty that I'll never forget my time with Lynn, or all the incredible things she made me feel.

Without a last name or contact info, I have nothing to grasp onto. My memories of her will have to be enough. I have to continue on with my life and make peace with the fact that I'll never see her again.

It's a sad thought, but I wouldn't take back his week for anything. Lynn was incredible and I had more fun with her than I thought possible. I'll cherish the memories we made together, and as much as I wish we could have had more time together, I'm grateful for the time we did have. Lynn will always have a place in my thoughts, and in my heart.

WANT to know what happens next? Keep reading for a sneak peek of Pucking Never!

# About Pucking Never

**WHAT IF YOU WANT TO BREAK THE RULES YOU'VE built your life around?**

LIFE POST-COLLEGE-GRADUATION IS TOUGH, especially living with my parents.

But I have goals, and my type A personality won't let me deviate.

So, when my pro hockey player twin brother asks me to manage his socials, I can't say no, despite loathing hockey and its players.

On my first day, I meet his best friend, Jensen—the guy I lost my virginity to.

One look and I know I'm in trouble.

Jensen is just as handsome as I remember and has one goal: making me his.

The problem? I have a rule: never date a hockey player.

And I never break a rule.

# Chapter One

## GRACE

As I stare at my brightly lit laptop screen, it seems to mock me. I'm supposed to be coming up with a list of ideas for online content to present to one of my clients, but I've got nothing. This isn't a normal problem for me. I typically have ideas flowing from my brain, but for some reason, I'm totally stuck today. I don't know why. There's no reason I shouldn't be cranking out pitch after pitch right now.

And yet, I'm grasping at straws.

Sitting back in my desk chair, I release a long, frustrated breath and pinch the bridge of my nose to try and fight back the headache that's drumming behind my eyes. What is wrong with me?

I'm Gracelynn-Freaking-Monroe. I don't get blocked.

Deciding I should just take a break, I shut my laptop and push to my feet. Looking around, I sigh. It probably doesn't help that I feel totally out of touch now that I'm back to living at home with my parents. It's all I can afford, though, as a recent college graduate with a budding (but not yet profitable) social media management business. My mom told me not to worry about it, that I can stay as long as I want. Still, I can't help but feel bad. I should be out there like everyone else, trying to make it in the world. But there isn't really anything I can do about that now, except to continue to save and hope that one day I'll have my own place.

And while I'm proud of my work and of the fact that I've landed a few loyal clients, as small as they might be, I feel... restless. Like I'm supposed to be doing something else. Something bigger. Something that will push my career to the heights I've always dreamed of.

For now, though, I need to be content, keep my head down, and pay my dues.

Making my way downstairs, I head to the kitchen. Perhaps a cup of tea will help to clear my thoughts so I can actually accomplish something., While I wait for it to whistle, I hop up onto the counter and sigh. I gaze up at the ceiling and wonder if I'm going to eat ramen or macaroni and cheese tonight. Suddenly, my phone buzzes.

I absentmindedly pick it up but then feel a jolt of surprise when I see that it's my brother, Carson. A frown crossing my face as I answer the call.

"Carson?"

"Hey, Gracie. How's Madison?"

I shrug, forgetting he can't see me, then answer, "It's fine. How's Denver?"

"Pretty great," he answers and I roll my eyes.

"Did you just call me to gloat about how great your life is going?" I grumble. "Because I warn you, I'm in no mood."

My handsome, charismatic, talented brother is living his best life while I'm scraping by, building my career bit-by-bit from the ground up. Carson is fulfilling his dream of playing professional hockey, and while I'm proud of him, I can't shake the shiver of jealousy crawling down my spine. He's always had things easier. At least, that's how it's always felt. I don't know if it's because he's been an athlete his whole life and people seem to practically worship him, but opportunities always just fall at his feet while I have to work my ass off to get anywhere in life.

Carson chuckles and says, "I promise, that's not why I called. Well, it's not the only reason I called. How's the social media business treating you?"

I furrow my brow. "It's fine. I've got some clients. Work is trickling in right now, but I'm getting my name out there and networking however I can. Things will pick up soon enough."

"What if I could help you?"

My frown deepens. "Help me? How?"

"I need a social media manager," Carson says. "What would you think of moving out here and working for me?"

Blinking, I sit frozen for several seconds, uncertain whether I heard him right or not.

"You...you want me to come work for you?" I murmur.

"Yeah," he replies. "Now that I've gone pro, my publicist says I need to represent myself more professionally online. You know I suck at that stuff, but you're brilliant. I'd pay you a steady salary and even provide some benefits. What do you think?"

I'm speechless. I hadn't expected anything like this when I answered my brother's call.

After several moments of silence on my part, Carson says, "Uh...Grace? You still there? Hello?"

"Oh!" I exclaim. "Sorry, I spaced out for a second. Um... are you sure you want me? You're not afraid this could be a conflict of interest or something?"

"Nah," he replies. "I want someone I know and trust for the job, and there aren't many people I trust more than you."

My lips curl into a small grin at that. Still, I continue to hesitate. It's not that I'm not interested in the job. I really am, and I know this could be an awesome opportunity for me. Being the social media manager for a professional athlete could catapult my career forward much further than I'd planned in such a short amount of time. Still, when I open my mouth to try and accept the job, the words get stuck in my throat.

Instead, I manage to say, "But, you know I hate hockey."

Carson releases a bark of laughter. "Yes, I'm aware of that, but come on, Gracie. You know this is a great opportunity for you and I don't want to hire a total stranger who doesn't understand me and what I'm all about. You just have to focus on my hockey career and no one else's. Plus, I'm not asking you to date any of the team, so you won't have to break your weird rule."

I roll my eyes at his teasing tone. "You know why I have that rule, Carson."

"Yeah, yeah," he groans. "I know, and trust me, I get it. My friends in high school were exactly that, high schoolers. Every single one of us had only one thing in mind, and that was exactly my reason for keeping you away from them. I also know what happened to Stacey was...messed up. But you can't really think all hockey players are assholes because of the way some teenagers acted a million years ago. What about me?"

"You are the one exception," I grumble.

My one rule of dating is that I don't date hockey players. Ever. People often laugh or think I'm joking if they find out my rule, but I'm dead serious about holding onto it. Throughout the years of being dragged along to my brother's hockey games and enduring his growing popularity as he got better and better, my experience with other hockey players has only ever been negative. It wasn't just how I was treated by them, though. I was actually left alone more often than not, because of Carson — but my friends weren't. They were treated like puck bunnies and never taken seriously. The hockey guys would always put their own wants and their careers before anything else. The image of my friend Stacey, tears streaming down her face as she held a pregnancy test in her hand, is burned into my mind.

I shake my head. Carson doesn't really know what happened with Stacey. He just thinks she was dumped before her asshole ex suddenly left our school. My naive brother has no idea that his former friend got Stacey pregnant and then abandoned her for greener hills.

Taking a deep breath, I give Carson my answer. "Alright, I'll do it. But if any of your teammates give me any trouble..."

"I'll keep 'em in check, don't worry," he replies with a note of seriousness in his voice that I'm not used to hearing. "You're taking a big step for me, Grace. I won't forget that."

"You're right about that," I assure him. "I won't let you."

My mind instantly flies to more stressful topics. The big one: am I even going to be able to afford rent? Denver is a big place, and—like most major cities—expensive. I ponder over my savings, and the money I currently have coming in from clients. Even though it's enough to get me going, if I lose a client... I won't make it.

"Hey, so... quick question." I say slightly stumbling across my words.

"What is it?"

Letting out a heavy sigh, I try to formulate my words without sounding more ridiculous than I feel. "How's housing there? I mean rent and that. I have to find a place to live—"

Laughter erupts through the phone quickly stopping me mid-sentence. "You don't need to worry about that."

"I don't? I mean, I'm pretty sure I need a place to live. I can't live with you."

"That's for sure." He snorts with amusement. "I mean, I'm going to put you in a place. I've got it covered. You're doing me a favor by agreeing in the first place. It's the least I can do."

My mind races with the information. I know he's my brother, but to do all of this for me... I don't even know how to feel. Taking a deep breath, I try to quiet my emotions. "Thank you... you have no idea how much that means to me."

"Don't mention it. Now, will you be able to keep your other clients if you move out here?" Carson asks.

I take a moment to think about that. There shouldn't be an issue. None of my clients require in-person meetings or anything like that. Everything's done online, so moving states shouldn't be a big deal. The only reason I moved back home to Madison after college was to save money on rent.

"Yeah," I answer. "That won't be a problem. I can manage their socials remotely and they'll be able to send me videos and images that I can edit. It'll be a smooth transition."

"Good." I can hear the smile in his voice. "You know I'm hopeless with any of that stuff, so I need you here, in-person."

"I know. It'll work out on my end, no worries."

"I'll owe you for this," he says. "I promise you won't regret this."

"All right. I'll talk to you later, Carson."

"Goodnight, Gracie."

After we hang up, I stare blankly at my silent phone for a long while. My life is about to change in ways I could have never anticipated, and all because of my goofy twin brother who happens to be good at hitting a puck with a stick.

Hopping off the counter, I stare at the already finished kettle as my chin drops into my hand. "What a day," I mutter to myself with a sigh. Moving into athlete territory is daunting. I didn't think I'd ever get pulled back into that world. All those countless hours of being dragged to Carson's games and dealing with the macho behavior of his teammates soured me toward the game even before my friends were ever affected by those assholes. The mere thought of willingly immersing myself in such an atmosphere makes my gut twist with unease.

But then again, this is a chance to expand my client base, to gain experience managing high-profile figures and their social media needs. I don't necessarily need to focus on the hockey aspect of things, really. Just the social media and the experience this is going to give me.

With a groan, I drop my head onto the counter and comb

my fingers through my hair. It takes some time for me to wrap my head around the magnitude of what accepting this job offer means for me. As I do so, however, I remind myself that this moment isn't just about a job opportunity or furthering my career, it's also about trust—the trust that Carson has placed in me.

I know he wouldn't put his career in my hands if he didn't believe I was capable of handling it. He knows how tough this decision is for me—how much I loathe the idea of becoming part of the hockey world—but he's still asking. That alone is enough to bolster my confidence and to quell some of the unease.

So, with a sudden surge of determination, I lift my head and pull out my phone once more to look up flight information to send to Carson.. The shiver of jealousy that had been plaguing me before is gone now, replaced by excitement and curiosity for what lies ahead.

The prospect of being Carson's social media manager is daunting, yes, but it's also thrilling. And despite my personal feelings about the game he loves so much, I can't help but feel a certain pride in my brother. He has always been exceptional, and now he has achieved his dream. And despite his success, he still remembered his somewhat antisocial sister back home who could do with a helping hand. For that, if nothing else, I can endure a little hockey in my life.

A FEW WEEKS LATER, I step off the plane in Denver, clutching my laptop bag in one hand and my phone in the other. I make my way through the arrival gate and look around to try and figure out where I need to go to find Carson. He said he'd meet me when I got here and take me to my new apartment, which he's gotten all arranged for me. I've got to say, so far the perks of working for my brother aren't too bad.

Following the flow of the crowd, I wander through the airport toward the baggage claim.

And as I approach the carousel, my eyes immediately spot Carson. He's hard to miss. Six feet tall and packed with muscle, he seems larger than life in the sea of people: a mountain among molehills. That said, looking at him is like looking in a mirror — that is if I were a man, and a giant — due to his identical blue eyes and the same dark brown hair with golden highlights. We've even got the same cowlick at the center of our foreheads. Warmth floods me at the sight of him. I have to admit, I've missed my goofy, puck-hitting, now-famous twin.

Carson spots me and his face breaks into a wide grin.

"Grace!" he calls over the crowds. He rushes over, pulling me into a bear hug that lifts me off my feet. "Welcome to Denver!" he exclaims as he sets me back down. His excitement is infectious and I feel a small surge of anticipation spark within me.

"Thanks, Carson," I reply, looking up at him. "It's good to see you."

"How was the flight?" he asks as we turn to the baggage carousel to wait for my bags.

"Good," I shrug. "Not too eventful."

He chuckles. "Well, I'm really glad you're here. This is going to be great, I promise."

I shoot him a grin. "I believe you, don't worry. I'm happy to be here, Carson."

He grabs my suitcases when they swing around the carousel and leads me out of the airport.

"The rest of your stuff already arrived," he told me. "I had it unpacked and set up in your new place, though I'm sure you'll rearrange it to your liking when you see it."

I laugh. "Oh, I'll probably rearrange it two or three times."

As soon as we step outside, the fresh mountain air hits me,

and I take in a deep breath and grin. We load my luggage into the back of his BMW, which is silver and sleek and clearly new. As Carson pulls out onto the highway, I take a moment to admire the city's skyline that comes into view against a backdrop of towering mountains, their peaks dusted with snow even though it's only early fall.

Carson was one of the few to get drafted right out of college, his feet never stepping a day into the pro minors. As soon as he finished his senior year, he was on a flight to Denver. The coach was, according to Carson, overly excited to snag him considering the perfect record he held for three years in a row. And though I did see my brother over the holidays, I haven't gotten a chance to check out his new life in Denver. Something I'd often wondered about, considering he is in the big leagues.

The drive to my new apartment is short, but awe-inspiring. Denver looks nothing like our hometown in Michigan. There are skyscrapers and busy streets filled with people rushing off to wherever they're headed. It's vibrant and lively – a stark contrast to our sleepy suburban neighborhood in Wisconsin. Less than a half hour later, Carson pulls into a sleek-looking apartment complex. I can't help but gape at the towering structure.

"This is where I'll be living?" I ask incredulously.

"Yep," he replies with an excited grin. "Same building as me. Welcome home, sis."

Carson helps me lug my suitcases up to the 12th floor where my apartment is located. The moment he swings open the door, I'm met with another surprise. The place is gorgeous—modern furniture, floor-to-ceiling windows offering stunning views of the city, and even a small kitchen that gleams with stainless steel appliances.

"Wow," is all I manage to utter as I walk further in, my suitcase wheels clicking against the polished wooden floor.

"I figured you'd need a comfortable place to work," Carson says from behind me. He seems pleased by my reaction. "Besides, if you're going to be managing social media for a professional athlete, you might as well live like one."

"I...this is just unbelievable, Carson," I stammer out. "Thank you."

There's a warmth in his gaze as he claps a heavy hand on my shoulder. "No need to thank me, Grace," he says sincerely. "You earned this. All of it."

In that moment, despite the lingering trepidation about my new job and the unfamiliar surroundings, I feel an unmistakable sense of belonging. Like I'm exactly where I'm supposed to be.

"Well," Carson says after a few moments. "I should let you settle in. We have a big day tomorrow. I want you to come to practice with me to take video. Sound good?"

"Sounds great," I tell him.

He reaches for me and pulls me into a tight hug, his big arms consuming me completely.

"I'm glad you're here," he murmurs. "I've missed you."

I wrap my arms around his waist and squeeze him back. "I've missed you too."

Pulling back, he looks down at me with a small smile and says, "All right. I'm on the fourteenth floor if you need anything, okay? I'll see you in the morning. Oh, and don't forget to call mom and tell her you got here safe and sound. She'll be blowing up my phone otherwise."

Soft laughter flows from me, as I nod. Our parents have been happily married for, well, god knows how long. The two of them are more in love than I've ever seen anyone, and honestly, it gives me hope. Hope that one day I will have the kind of relationship they do. Which means my standards are high, because I've seen the kind of relationships some of my friends have had, and I won't settle for less when it comes to looking for love. Not that falling in love is anywhere on my radar right now.

"I will, don't worry," I assure him, patting his arm. "I'm just going to get unpacked and relax so I'm ready to hit the ground running tomorrow."

He seems hesitant to leave, but I walk him to the door and he tells me goodbye one more time before leaving to go to his own apartment. I shut the door behind him and turn around to press my back against it and release a long breath. Okay. I'm here. I'm doing this. Pushing away from the door, I cross the apartment to the large windows and stare out at the cityscape. My heart begins to race with excitement and my lips curl into a wide smile.

This is my new life, and despite my hang-ups about hockey, I'm actually looking forward to seeing where this new chapter takes me.

CLICK HERE TO download Pucking Never today!

# Afterword

Thank you so much for taking the time to read this book. I hope you have enjoyed this escape from reality.

.

# About the Author

Want to know what happens next? Sign up for my newsletter!

Author bio:

Hello, I'm Katie Strong, a California dreamer who's been soaking up the ocean breeze since birth. Life's been a wild ride, especially raising my fiercely independent son.

When I'm not navigating the highs and lows of motherhood, you'll find me lost in the world of writing. Words are my sanctuary, my escape, where I can explore the depths of passion and desire.

But when the laptop closes, I trade the keyboard for a crochet hook. There's just something soothing about the meditative rhythm of creating stitches, a way to unwind and make something beautiful with my own two hands.

I hope you enjoy my books and join me on this journey where love and creativity collide, where every page turned and every stitch woven brings us closer to the heart of what truly matters.

Printed in Great Britain
by Amazon